THIS WALKER BOOK BELONGS TO:

_____

_____

_____

_____

D0488666

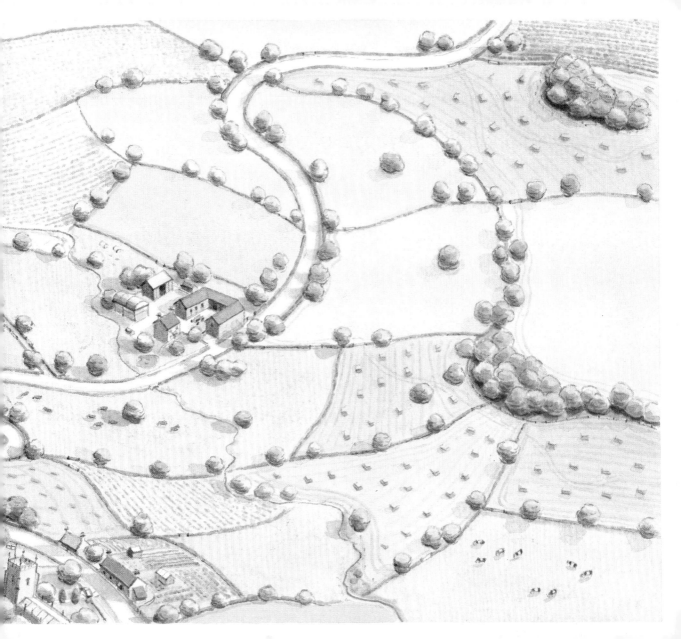

For Ali Bateman   H.M.

For my mother and father   N.J.

With thanks to farmer Richard Aldous
for his technical assistance

First published 1986 by
Walker Books Ltd
87 Vauxhall Walk
London SE11 5HJ

This edition published 1990

Printed and bound in Italy by L.E.G.O., Vicenza

British Library Cataloguing in Publication Data
Maisner, Heather
Jack and the combine.—(The tractors of Thomson's Yard)
I. Title   II. Johnson, Norman   III. Series
823'.914 [J]   PZ7
ISBN 0-7445-1438-X

JACK
AND THE COMBINE

WRITTEN BY

HEATHER MAISNER

ILLUSTRATED BY

NORMAN JOHNSON

WALKER BOOKS
LONDON

On the first day of the harvest Jack began to sing as soon as Farmer Thomson and his daughter Rosemary fitted the cutting and threshing machine to his back. The animals and tractors watched him set off down the drive.

'I wish I were cutting the fields again,' sighed Sam, the old tractor.

'So do I,' croaked Rufus, the cart-horse. 'I used to love harvest time.'

'I hate it,' moaned Kate, the red tractor. 'I get so tired and Jack works much too fast.'

Out in the main road Jack kept close to the hedge. He went past the sugar-beet and by the forest, round the pond, through the gate and into the field.

They watched Jack set off down the drive.

Then up and down and up and down he drove, cutting the corn and threshing the corn, and singing his song as he went:

> 'I'm a tractor, my name is Jack,
> I live in Thomson's Yard.
> I can go forward and I can go back,
> I'm happiest working hard.'

'Do slow down,' Kate panted behind him. 'I'll never keep up with the bales.'

'Of course you will,' laughed Jack.

'I'm hot and sore and covered with midges,' she said.

'Sing and you'll soon forget,' said Jack.

'Do slow down,' Kate panted.

By evening the field was dotted with bales. Aching and tired, the tractors crawled back to the yard.

'Tomorrow we start over the hill,' said Jack.

'Oh no.' Kate's eyes began to close. 'I wish I could sleep for a week.'

'I wish I could work all night,' said Jack. But soon he too fell asleep.

CRUNCH   CRUNCH   CRUNCH

Jack opened one eye. It was still dark.

CRUNCH   CRUNCH   CRUNCH

'What is it?' Kate whispered, pressing against him. An enormous thing was moving down the drive.

   'What is it?' Kate whispered.

'It's the end of the world,' groaned Sam.

'Cock-a-doodle-doo! Cock-a-doodle-doo!' cried the cockerel. The cart-horse neighed and stamped his hoofs. The pigs snorted, the cows mooed. The dog ran out into the drive and howled. But the monster moved steadily towards them.

CRUNCH   CRUNCH   CRUNCH

Jack stepped boldly forward.
'Stop!' he said. 'Who are you? What do you want?'

The monster stood still and licked its lips. Its nostrils flared. It opened its mouth and a voice boomed out.
'I'm Harold, Harold the combine.
I've come to cut Farmer Thomson's corn.'
The farmyard was silent.
'That's my job,' said Jack. 'I cut the corn.'
'Was your job,' said the combine. 'Now it's mine.'

‘Stop,’ Jack said. ‘Who are you?’

When the sun was high in the sky, Harold moved down the drive with Farmer Thomson.

'He hasn't got a scratch on him,' said Kate. 'He probably doesn't know how to cut the fields.'

'Oh, yes I do,' said Harold. 'I can do everything.' He swung out into the main road and his body filled the whole space from one side to the other.

Along the main road and past the sugar-beet, by the forest and round the pond, up the hill and through the gate he lurched.

Then up and down and up and down he rolled, cutting and threshing and cleaning the corn.

❧ *Harold's body filled the whole road.* ❧

Back at the yard Jack stood silently. For the first time in his life he hadn't sung his song.

'You can do my job,' whispered Kate. 'You can do the baling.'

'I expect Harold does that too,' said Jack. 'I guess I'll be sitting in the yard all day now, unless I'm sold for scrap.' A large tear rolled down his cheek. 'Trouble is, I don't know what to do if I'm not working.'

Suddenly Rosemary ran up the drive and began to fit the large trailer to Jack. Without saying a word they set off for the fields.

A large tear rolled down Jack's cheek.

Along the road and past the sugar-beet, by the forest and round the pond, up the hill and through the gate they hurried.

Harold stood absolutely still in the middle of the field. He'd stopped working.

'What's up?' asked Jack. 'Why have you stopped?'

'The grain needs emptying,' said Harold.

'Can't you take care of that yourself?' asked Jack.

'Of course not,' Harold snorted. 'I'm needed here. I can't go trundling back to the yard every twenty minutes, can I?'

'Why have you stopped?' asked Jack.

As the grain spilt from Harold's tank into the trailer, Jack asked, 'What do you do after the harvest, Harold, when all the corn's cut?'

'Nothing. I rest.'

'You mean you don't do anything all year?'

'That's right. I preserve my energy for the harvest.'

Jack moved back along the road with the trailer full of corn. If Harold spent most of the year resting, he wouldn't be taking Jack's place after all. There was the ploughing and hedge-cutting, the digging and shovelling, the fetching and carrying and oh so many things to do. Slowly he began to sing:

> 'I'm a tractor, my name is Jack,
> I live in Thomson's Yard.
> I can go forward and I can go back,
> I'm happiest working hard.'

Slowly Jack began to sing.

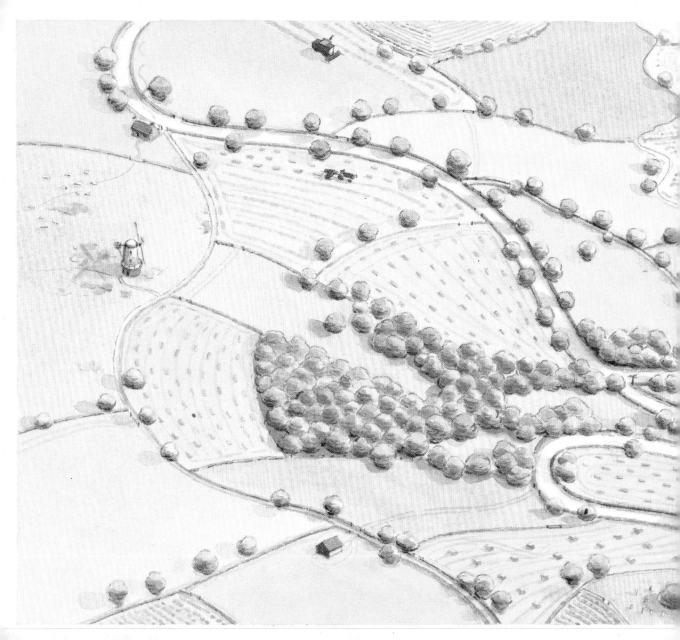

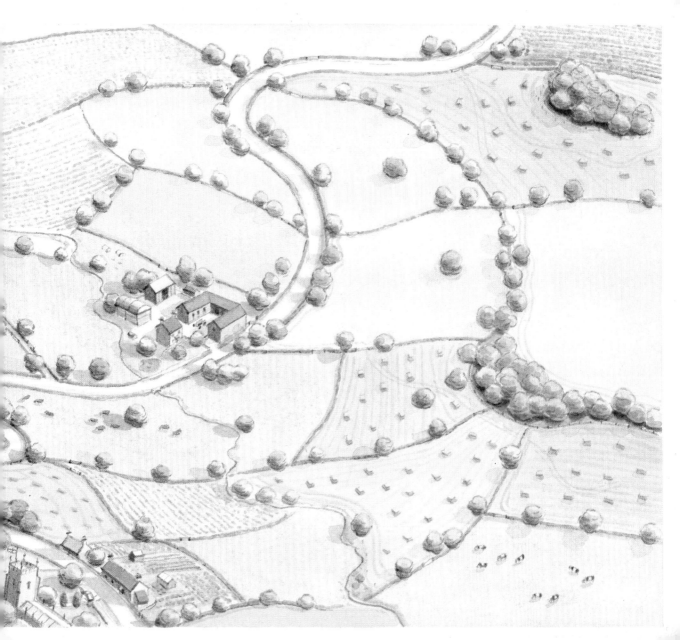

MORE WALKER PAPERBACKS
For You to Enjoy

KATE AND THE CUTTER
by Heather Maisner/Norman Johnson

Another title in the Tractors of Thomson's Yard series. It's winter and hedge-cutting time – and Kate races the neighbour's arrogant tractor Len to see who can finish first!

ISBN 0-7445-1439-8 £1.99

MACHINES AT WORK
by Gaynor Chapman

Two colourful and absorbing studies of machines at work – drills and water-pumps, excavators and backhoe loaders, concrete mixers, mobile cranes and many more.

ISBN 0-7445-0916-5 ROAD WORKS £2.99
ISBN 0-7445-0917-3 BUILDING WORKS £2.99

Walker Paperbacks are available from most booksellers, or by post from Walker Books Ltd, PO Box 11, Falmouth, Cornwall TR10 9EN.

To order, send:

Title, author, ISBN number and price for each book ordered
Your full name and address
Cheque or postal order for the total amount, plus postage and packing:

UK, BFPO and Eire – 50p for first book, plus 10p for
each additional book to a maximum charge of £2.00.
Overseas Customers – £1.25 for first book,
plus 25p per copy for each additional book.

Prices are correct at time of going to press, but are subject to change without notice.